Poems & Butterflies

A gift of Inspirational Poems
For every occasion.
An insight into the world of a Poet.

For Greg, Bonnie & Clyde — my whole world.

For Dad — who always said I could with pride in his voice.

And for Jim — who makes me feel like one of his own.

Welcome to my world.
Where poems are my style.
Of showing you how I feel.
And to make you smile.

I hope you find a verse.
That will brighten up your day.
And take it as my gift
To help you on your way.

With Love
Louise

Chapters

- _Family & Friendship_

- _Love & Marriage_

- _Grief & Sorrow_

- _Health & Stress_

- _For the Children_

- _Holidays & Celebrations & New Journeys_

- _Religious & Spiritual_

- _Other Moments_

Always believe in the beauty of Butterflies & the power of Fairies.
They help to make life more enchanting.

Family & Friendship

My Friend

When life is too much,
And you just want to hide.
I'll be there every day,
Right by your side.

When dreams are like stars,
Too high to touch.
I swear I'll find a way,
I love you that much.

Cause when I was lost,
In a starless night.
You were right there,
Fighting my fights.

You always believed,
In my dreams that could be.
You simply took my hand,
And were there for me.

So, when you feel
Life gets too tough.
And that hope in tomorrow
Isn't enough.

I'll get you through today,
One step at a time.
And when that road is steep,
Together we will climb.

And I know how hard
The rain can feel.
When heartache is so bad,
It's almost unreal.

And I know that a friend
Can make the sun shine.
And I thank God every day
That you are mine.

So, I write this for you,
To let you know.
I'm here night and day,
I'll never let go.

You have a friend,
That will always see.
The amazing woman
I know you to be.

L.M Haddow

My Husbands Arms

Your arms they are my strength.
When life is not being kind.
They take me to a safer place.
And help me to unwind.

Your arms are where I am.
Where I truly belong.
In them I am loved so dear.
All rights change from wrong.

In your arms I know I'm led.
To be my own true self.
There is no other place for me.
Your arms are my whole wealth.

Your arms around me feel so right.
I am safe and sound and free.
Where else could I have such warmth?
There is no place for me.

Thank you for holding me.
When life was just a strain.
Your love for me is all around.
You lessen all my pain.

My husband, in your arms.
I will live forever more.
I love you with all my heart.
Love you and adore.

L.M Haddow

My wish for you

May your adventure be as special,
And fabulous as you.
May your journey to tomorrow,
Be easy and true.

May you find all your dreams,
And hopes to be real.
May you face each new day,
With love and pure zeal.

May the sunshine always,
Keep you warm.
May you always have shelter,
From any storm.

May love be your greatest,
Valuable in life.
May your heart remain open,
Even in strife.

May your happiness continue,
As the years embark.
May you always quest,
For the light in the dark,

May you always remain,
The joyous person I know.
May your visions for the future,
Prosper and grow.

L.M Haddow

Kindred Garden

The family is a seed of the soul.
Like a Garden it needs love to grow.
With every root, flower and vine.
Rises and shifts through-out time.

Roses that bloom clear and bright.
Sweet pink blossoms so small and light.
Trees that stand above them all.
Leaves of colour free to fall.

Each branch can offer a calm retreat.
Each corner gives warmth and heat.
Where ladybirds can go and hide.
Is a place of peace, love and pride.

Where no matter, come rain or snow.
The seeds are always safe to grow.
Where roots can never be removed.
And days of past can be renewed.

And in each yard of young and old.
Is the Gardener strong and in control.
Who tends the shrubs and guides the way.
Through Winter, Summer, come what may.

For each flower, fern and shoot.
That guiding hand is the vital fruit.
To tend with grace, love and charm.
Protecting all, safe from harm.

The sun that keeps the seedling alive.
The rain that helps the grass to thrive.
The one that all most can depend.
The Mother, the Father and the friend.

L.M Haddow

Thank you

Thanks, is such a little word.
And it rarely is enough.
For someone who is kind to you,
When Life is especially rough.

When someone goes out their way,
To just show you that they care.
To hold your hand and be your friend.
And help to ease despair.

And often when life kicks you,
You find on whom you can depend.
Who steps up and is by your side,
Who is your true, real, friend!

And with this act of kindness.
It is impossible to portray.
What a difference it can make,
And uplift an arduous day.

Just to have some small support,
Or a moment of understanding.
To know that when there is pain in life,
Steps are often demanding.

So, thank you for being so generous,
In both your love and time.
You help to ease my trying days.
And lessen the slope I climb.

Please know that if you ever,
Need a friend to help you stand.
I will always be right there for you.
Just please - hold out your hand.

L.M Haddow

Perfect Gold

The funny thing about friendship,
It can be a little like life.
Ups and downs, laughter and tears,
Moments of trouble and strife.

But today I want to tell you,
And please know that this is true.
My life is truly blessed,
Because I have a friend in you.

You are a strong and beautiful woman,
With a heart of perfect gold.
I can never be alone in life;
Your hand is there to hold.

And I know I don't always tell you,
And for this I am to blame.
But I am a better person,
For simply knowing your name.

Your friendship means more
Than all the world to me.
Without you in my life,
I wouldn't know how to be.

Always been a constant,
In times good and bad.
Never letting me lose myself,
Either when happy or sad.

I also want to let you know,
Though I hope you are aware.
That no matter what is in my life,
For you I'm always there.

I would climb whatever mountain,
Is causing you any pain.
And will hold your hand for all my life
Come both sun and rain.

So, thank you for our friendship.
The other half of my soul.
Our friendship will endure forever.
For all of time, I know.

L.M Haddow

<u>Cherished Friends</u>

What does Friendship mean?
For me it is my link.
To love and peace, truth and joy.
A rope to stop me sink.

Friendship comes when times are hard
But also, in moments of cheer.
A friend is one that calms your nerves.
And lessens times of fear.

Friends always take the time.
To be your guiding light.
Someone who is by your side.
When the sun is crossed by night.

Cherish that friend that holds your hand.
And the words of truth they say.
Never doubt their love for you.
Or their guidance on your way.

L.M Haddow

Our Kitty Cat Babies

What would I do without you?
My precious furry friends.
Full of fun, and such a blessing.
And loving to the end.

You look to me with eyes of love.
And cuddle me with joy.
My perfect little fur babies.
My sweet Girl and boy.

It seems your greatest prize in life,
Is being so close to me.
I think God knew how comforting,
Your warm, soft fur would be.

And for me I know that you,
Have been sent from up above.
You have filled that empty void I had.
And turned it into love.

The Love we share forever.
Never are we apart.
And you, my babies, will always have.
Paw prints in my heart.

L.M Haddow

Always Lesa

My best friend is amazing.
She has a wonderous smile.
She always sees the best.
When life is running wild.

She held me in dark moments.
And drank my health a lot.
She sees the best within me.
And un-tangles every knot.

My best friend is my family.
I've known her all my days.
She stands beside me always.
And never loses way.

She never lets me down.
She always has my back.
She knows my faults and loves me.
Her faith, it does not lack.

So, my best friend I always,
Will love and need close by.
And I pray that when she needs me.
I will calm her any cry.

L.M Haddow

The Polloks (without the "C")

My Family is a strange one.
We can be distant and obtuse.
We tend not to talk well.
Goes back generations if you want the truth.

We're not big on feelings.
We'll argue black is white.
And no matter what the evidence.
Be Dammed if we aren't right.

We tend to hold a grudge.
Often to our peril.
And we don't always compromise.
Or share our feelings well.

The Pollok clan I must admit.
Can be sometimes as it seems.
Arrogance and a fighting spirit
Seems the running theme.

But amongst our may cons.
There are bits that people forget.
We are fiercely loyal, true friends.
And never forget a debt.

We can create works of art.
Talents that we share.
And we're humble in our gifts.
No matter how they fair.

We stand for what we believe in.
And never shy from a fight.
The courage of our convictions
Tends to keep us right.

Not ones to call each other.
Or visit at our homes.
But when the chips are down.
You'll find us in our droves.

So, when you judge on sight.
The arrogance we can display.
Remember if we're on your team
We're on your team to stay.

The memberships forever.
In our crazy Highland Clan.
And I for one am proud.
A Pollok is who I am.

L.M Haddow

I saw yesterday a Butterfly.
It made my heart take flight.

Love & Marriage

May all that glitters be gold

There is no beginning of love.
Just as there is no end.
There is only the moment you know.
You have found your lover and friend.

And the journey of life, the paths that we take,
Bring moments we cherish and treasure.
Memories are made, passion and joy.
Scenes of wonder and pleasure.

So today as you start your new chapter in life.
And take each other hands to hold.
May your journey into tomorrow be filled with peace.
And may all that glitters be gold.

L.M Haddow

<u>Wedding Kiss</u>

To have and to hold,
To love and treasure.
Memories to be made,
Moments of pleasure.

Dreams of tomorrow
With lessons from the past.
A new day together
With passion to last.

Blessings and journeys.
Still to be deemed.
Joy and peace.
In dreams to be dreamed.

May today be full of,
Love and bliss.
And your future sealed,
With your wedding kiss.

L.M Haddow

Butterflies appear

Some say that love is blinding,
It can make you lose your way.
They say that it's a battle.
That is what they say.

They tell me that I should,
Protect my heart, be strong.
And never let me lose myself.
Know what's right, what's wrong.

And yes, their words are clear,
And make a lot of sense.
I should always keep on watch.
Always have defence.

But then I tend to wonder.
How bleak their life must be?
Never to of felt or had,
That love that sets you free.

The kind of love that keeps you,
Far from sleep at night.
The love that makes you sing,
The love that makes you fight.

That feeling of despair,
When you leave a room.
The butterflies appear,
Knowing I will see you soon.

The spark of wonderous passion,
That comes from just a sigh.
The joy of true excitement.
To look deep in your eyes.

Yes, my love is blinding.
I want the world to know.
You taught me to laugh and cry.
To let a little go.

You make me feel so safe,
So, defence is not required.
Loved and cherished always,
Precious and desired.

I don't want to fight it.
I am happy to be lost.
Open up my heart to you.
And love you at all cost.

L.M Haddow

<u>*Wedding Blessing*</u>

Today you stand with love all around.
Our blessings to you from our hearts.
May you find joy and passion as you hold hands.
As this new journey in life now starts.

May the delight of today carry on.
And tomorrow bring you true peace.
May life bring you passion and bliss.
May hardships forever now cease.

To have and to hold from this day through.
With moments of wonder and pleasure.
May memories of yesterday stay in your heart.
And new dreams now begin to treasure.

L.M Haddow

My first ever Poem to Greg

Finding the words, I want to say.
Is not a task I find easy each day.
And even though they are in my heart.
I often don't know how to start.

And I know I often find doubt and worry.
My feelings seem vague and sometimes blurry.
I struggle sometimes to believe and trust.
But I know my concerns are very unjust.

Because when I am dark and scare of the pain.
There isn't a moment that you question the strain.
You stand by our love and all that we share.
With no question or doubt or despair.

You truly believe and are simply there.
To fight for us and show that you care.
And you hold my hand, even when we're apart.
And ensure I know the love in your heart.

And that's a gift I cherish from you.
In all that you give, believe and do.
You make me feel safe and feel free.
You hold my heart, as you hold me.

Through this poem I hope you will know.
I will always love you and will never let go.

L.M Haddow

My Sister on my Wedding Day

When we were little we used to play.
At dressing up and our wedding day.
And some years ago, beside you I stood.
And watched as you married a man true and good.

And now big Sister - my turn has come.
To marry the man, I know is the one.
But even though I love him true.
I couldn't get married, without you.

Standing beside me as I become his wife.
Just as you've done for all off my life.
Helping me get through my special day.
Making it perfect in every way.

And so, to you My Sister - this I send.
Not just my Sister – also my Friend.
And ask on our Day - I hope you will be.
My Matron of Honour, standing right beside me.

L.M Haddow

<u>*Sunrise*</u>

In the morning when you wake,
A precious hand to hold.
If the future is uncertain,
Comforting words to be told.

The love that you have gathered,
Through the time of loves great sphere.
Will see you through tomorrow.
And always hold you near.

So, blessings on this day.
And all the days to arrive.
May your devotion forever cherish you,
With every new sunrise.

L.M Haddow

My Engagement poem to Greg

You asked me a question – a precious thing,
Down on one knee – and sealed with a ring.
To stand by you – and become your wife.
To give you my heart for the rest of my life.

You made a promise that you would always be,
Loving and caring - and ever there for me.
You took my hand and stole my heart,
And promised me, we would never part.

And now we plan – with joy and pride,
For the day you're a groom and I your bride.
The time is busy, for the day to come,
Filled with rushing - to get things done.

And yes, we both want, our day to be right,
From the holy chapel - to the party at night.
But for me - and I say this out loud,
The one thing that matters, that makes me proud.

Is that when I walk in my brand-new dress.
And all the details have been laid to rest.
The music is perfect and so are the flowers.
There'll be one thing for me that overpowers.

The man that waits with his charming smile,
For me at the end of that long, long aisle.
Will be you my Darling with all your affection,
Offering me love and all your protection.

So, a pre-wedding vow - this I promise,
To always be true and always be honest.
I will stand by your side now and forever.
Come what may – I will leave you never.

So, let's look to our future as Husband and Wife.
With moments of Joy and moments of strife.
Together - I know we can handle it all,
Cause we will catch each other when we fall.

L.M Haddow

The river

The river of life you have travelled together.
With blessings, hopes and dreams.
You have filled each other's lives which such joy.
Given with comfort, protection and means.

Today you begin a chapter brand new.
With the love that surrounds both your hearts.
New passions and journeys still to discover.
As this new road you now walk starts.

May blessing's find you today and always.
May your love for each other leave you never.
And when tomorrow begins with a brand-new sunrise.
May your joy and peace last forever.

L.M Haddow

<u>*Hand to hold*</u>

I wonder what my life would be.
Without you standing next to me.
Without your hand to hold in mine.
Without your arms for all of time.

My heart it drops when I think of a life.
In you're not my Husband or I your wife.
All my tomorrow's I know quite true.
Would be drab and lonely if I didn't have you.

You bring to my life a whole new dream.
Where life is not as dark as it seems.
I am free and content and safe as I am.
Cause I am your lady and you are my man.

So, on this day I wish you to know.
Every day, my love continues to grow.
My gift to you always and forever.
Is to stand by you and leave you never.

L.M Haddow

Our Bubble

In our bubble there is cat hair.
And we must go up a flight of stairs.
Our bubble has a few odd stains
And that boiler brings a lot of pains.

The roof may need a bit of work.
And in the oven things do lurk.
It's not a castle of that I'm sure.
And the furniture may seem poor.

The cats they live as if the owned.
Their toys are just as they'd thrown.
And the draft that comes from down the loft.
Am pretty sure caused that cough.

Our bubble in winter is freezing cold.
And in summer the heat makes us fold.
It creaks and groans every day.
And it may even stand in our way.

But in our bubble, this I feel.
It's a place to me where life is real.
You and me and our two cats.
Love and peace, rows and spats.

When we close the door at night.
Even when the days been shite.
We are together safe and sound.
Just us four, with love around.

About the cracks I worry not.
Or even if the walls do rot.
Cause our love has strength all its own.
And I love our bubble, our perfect home.

L.M Haddow

Tender Touch

A single kiss, a tender touch.
A moment that time stands still.
A loving look, a gentle sigh.
Excitement and the thrill.

Love it captures you from the first.
It holds you tight around.
It gives you joy and yes, some doubt.
But all barriers, it breaks down.

Take this love that you have found.
And guard it with your heart.
May the joy of today always stay.
And all your dreams now start.

L.M Haddow

I believe the spirits of my Loved ones.
Fly beside the Butterflies.

Grief & Sorrow

<u>Sunshine</u>

Sunshine comes to us once a while.
A joyous person to make us smile.
One that brings every single day.
Friendship and love in every way.

As if a gift given – they enter our being.
Showering peace – calming and freeing.
And then they become part of our soul.
Completing us and making us whole.

Then storm clouds can gather and bring the rain.
There nothing to say to ease the pain.
One feels when the sun has been taken away.
Or fill the void now left every day.

Thinking of the sun – through memories so dear.
Though painful to remember the warmth so clear.
But Little bits and pieces of the days lived as one.
The happy times and joy of moments in the sun.

And though words are lost, and nothing can be said.
To ease the hurt - and moments of dread.
Please do know that even, when feeling alone.
You are loved and thought of and never on your own.

There are family there to try and warm the cold.
And many hands, for you, always to hold.
Prayers are with you, and all our affection.
Offering support and all our protection.

So please when times - are too hard to bear.
Hold out your hand – we will always be there.
And though we cannot replace the light.
We will stand by your side, to help fight your fight.

L.M Haddow

<u>*Our Angel Daughter*</u>

Our Darling Angel Daughter,
That was with us for a while.
You had your Fathers strength,
And his lovely smile.

We had some time to hold you,
And kiss your face so sweet.
We cherish all those moments,
And thank God he let us meet.

But Heaven wanted an Angel.
And you were needed there.
And even though we wanted you,
We knew we had to share.

When others look to the heavens,
They see stars shinning bright.
But we see you amongst them,
Playing within their light.

We love you so very dearly,
We miss you every day.
But we know that you are near us,
Just a cloud away.

And we know that our loved ones,
In heaven next to you,
Will cuddle you for all of time.
Till we get there too.

So, play safe our Angel Daughter.
Always with our Love.
Be forever Beautiful,
In the stars above.

L.M Haddow

<u>*Don't cry for me forever*</u>

I lived each day my way.
I stood for all I knew.
I made mistakes yes, I know.
But I always saw it through.

I was not always perfect.
I hope I caused no pain.
Know that I am sorry.
If I gave you any strain.

So, as you say goodbye.
And perhaps your grief is strong.
Please know that I am happy.
Safe where I belong.

Don't cry for me forever.
That is not my way.
Know that I am with you,
Close by you every day.

L.M Haddow

The honour of grief

Shadows don't define us.
When grief is in our way.
Darkness is not the only,
Sense we feel today.

Here we gather together.
To say our final farewell.
And though our hearts are heavy.
We share memories we can tell.

Moments that we lived.
With our loved one who has gone.
Joy and grace, peace and dreams.
In us he does live on.

So, grief it may be a burden.
And we wish it wasn't true.
But to feel the grief you must feel love.
So, grief is an honour on you.

You spent those days and journeys.
Walked with him through life.
The privilege of holding his hand.
In moments of joy and strife.

And I for one am honoured.
To say I mourn this day.
Because I got to know his love.
And I miss him, I can say.

L.M Haddow

John's Water Colours

A lonely vessel sails.
To meet her final wave.
The sea a stormy, forbidden void.
To take as much as save.

And in the darken waters
Waves rush to caress the sand
We say our final farewell.
To our Dear sea loving man.

His canvas now complete.
The painting of his day.
Yet the colours that he gave us.
Will forever stay.

So as the tide recedes.
We know he is not gone.
For though his vessel leaves us.
His painting will live on.

L.M Haddow

Take my Soul

The day they said you were gone.
I told them that they lied.
That you had said you were mine.
Until the sun did not rise.

I said that we would always be
Forever close in heart
That never would you be far away.
That our hands would never part.

But they said the words quite clear
And my tears were flowing free
So, if they lie why would I
Be feeling lost at sea?

I don't know how to be alone.
I am afraid of the night.
I need your hand close to mine.
I need you in my sight.

But my love if you must go.
Then take with you my soul.
It belongs to you from the day we met
And with you it's only whole.

Until the day we meet again.
I know that day will descend.
But I will always stay so true.
As your lover and your friend.

L.M Haddow

New start

Grief is not always,
Just reserved for death.
One feels it in the moments,
Dreams are laid to rest.

It can be found amongst us,
Through-out our every day.
A friend that no longer see's us,
Or a lover who lost their way.

But grief, it is a part,
Of life that we must face.
It makes us stronger always,
It gives us rules to trace.

Lessons that we learn.
Because of what we lost.
Should always be treasured,
And remembered at all cost.

Take your grief with love.
Combine them in your heart.
Never forget the journey that was.
And start your brand-new start.

L.M Haddow

Lonely place

I stand here waiting
To see your smiling face.
I can't believe I am leaving you,
In this lonely place.

It seems a dream in motion.
A nightmare from the start.
My hopes are all but broken.
My soul is torn apart.

Will you feel afraid,
Without me by your side?
Is the darkness freeing,
Are you taking it in your stride?

I walk without touching.
The ground in which you lay.
My heart is no longer with me.
It's with you so far away.

And I know you are shouting.
"Be strong and be brave".
But my Dear, how can I?
I am standing at your grave.

Tomorrow seems so pointless.
Though I know I will find a way.
Each step I take with pain,
My burdens heavy weigh.

So, stay close to me my Darling.
Though I leave you so.
Keep your arms around me.
And ease my sorrow woe.

L.M Haddow

Mum

You took my hand when times were tough.
You said a prayer filled with love.
You held me close when I could not see.
You let me cry but were there for me.

You never said I could not do.
You simply said, "I believe in you".
You never let me lose my self.
You always saw my inner wealth.

You never told me not to run.
You never stopped me having fun.
You stood behind and watched me go.
You waited till I needed you so.

You told me off in some crazy fight.
You still made sure I was kissed goodnight.
You watched me grow from then to now.
You never took that well deserved bow.

You are the woman I aim to be.
You are the best that I can see.
You are my Mother, my loving friend.
You carried me with you, till the end.

You will always be in my heart
Your love I know will not depart.
Your love is in me and all I do.
I am who I am, because of you.

L.M Haddow

I never got to cuddle you

I never got to cuddle you.
Or hold you in my arms.
I never saw your eyes in mine
Or see your precious charms.

I carried you inside me
I loved you from the start
But you were meant to be an Angel
And we too early had to part

I cry a lot over you
And miss you next to me
But I know that you are above
Playing, strong and free.

Only I remember you.
There is no grave to mark you here.
But know my Darling baby
To me you are so dear.

A mummy I feel I am
With my Child far away.
But I know I will be with you.
Somehow on some day.

So, Darling please know
That even if apart.
My love for you will never end.
I carry you in my heart.

L.M Haddow

The beauty of a Butterfly.
Can bring joy to your heart.

Health & Stress

Rainbow

The time requires a rainbow.
And an angel as my guide.
To see me through the days of mist,
And wipe the tears I cried.

The dawn it seems to be hiding,
And the fog has hindered my way.
Each step is slow and painful,
The darkness never turning to day.

And each path I walk is daunting.
No comfort and peace on my trail.
Dreaming of some new shelter,
From the rain and freezing gale.

And silently I hold each moment,
Wishing for that rainbow to grow.
For the mist to clear and leave me,
For the sunshine to ultimately show.

And to make it back to the daylight.
Hope the dawn can again be my own.
And step within the sun's warm sparkle,
To find the rainbow has flourished and grown.

So, I hold on to the longings,
And wait for the storm to fade.
And search each day for the rainbow,
To help end this aching crusade.

And if tomorrow arrives with more weariness,
May I keep in my heart the will?
To remember that to walk is a blessing,
To walk in pain and still smile - is a skill.

L.M Haddow

Through my eyes

How does the world see me?
Now that my life has evolved?
Does my smile no longer please you?
Or do my sticks cause that to dissolve?

Do you see my pain in each step?
Or is my slowness to you a bother?
Do I trouble your busy lifestyle?
Are my limits to you in-proper?

I see the world now so strangely,
In a way I never could expect.
Colours to me seem darker
My dreams are now all but wrecked.

But each step I take is a victory.
And despite my pain I walk tall.
You can laugh or sigh if you need to
But be sure I get up when I fall.

My words are still strong and keen.
And though I may seem to you weak
But know every time you taunt me
My strength is to turn the other cheek.

So, while you may think me a hassle.
I no longer care about your view.
My life is filled with such love
That all sympathies I have lie with you.

L.M Haddow

The ladder

The ladder is high and foreboding.
There is no aid to help you climb.
The top is covered in darkness,
And moments seem to cease in time.

The clouds never nearer they come.
Yet no choice have you to continue.
Life depends on each step you take,
It all lies on the strength within you.

Whispers and voices, you hear,
Though not a word really makes sense.
Your mind and heart are in shadows,
And the loneliness you feel, immense.

But to climb is the only real path
No other route for you is there.
And despite the fear and the worry,
You must fight through the joyless despair.

And hands may reach out and touch you.
But their warmth is a brief reprieve.
They don't see the true burden you carry.
And your smile does only deceive.

With each step the darkness comes closer,
And the urge to fall back is strong.
But each step you must take is a moment.
That is part of your story and song.

L.M. Haddow

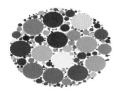

<u>Do you serve Cocktails?</u>

I used to ask when I went out.
The hotel or the bar.
Do you serve Cocktails?
And do you have a Spa?

Now my world has altered.
And changes must be made.
I now must utter words.
That make me feel afraid.

Do you have easy access?
Are the toilets on first floor?
Are you disabled friendly?
I must sound such a bore!

But when each day's a challenge.
In a way that was never hoped
Agendas change, as do questions.
You must learn you have to cope.

To me just getting dressed.
Is a hurdle I do find.
To tie my shoes or brush my hair.
Is now in life a grind.

If I could jump back.
20 years or more.
I would tell my healthy self.
Stand up and do explore.

Take pleasure in your walking.
See all there is to see.
Live out each adventure.
Swim in every sea.

Have fun and drive your car.
Or stay out a bit too late.
To watch a movie or see a friend.
To not worry about your weight.

Never take for granted.
Health you have by chance
Climb each hill before you.
Run and skip and dance.

Cause in a single moment.
It all can disappear.
When the little things you used to do.
Become moments full of fear.

And keep inside you always.
That life can sometimes tilt.
The dreams you have constructed.
Can crumble once they're built.

So always keep a smile.
In your heart when you are strong.
Never forget how blessed you are.
Or forget to sing your song.

L.M Haddow

At rest

When the world is fast asleep.
And the day turns into night.
Only shadows around do creep.
And stars shine so bright.

When all is quiet and very still.
When you think the worlds at peace.
Not one sound, din or thrill
When all busy times have ceased.

When your body is meant to rest.
And dreams are so exciting.
For me there starts a harder test.
Pain that is horrifically biting.

Hours are long when night arrives.
Tears seem to flow more free.
And it seems tougher to survive
When dark thoughts come over me.

In the night I always find
My pain seems arduous more.
The moments seem to slowly grind.
Each tear can be honestly sore.

But in the gloom, I often observe,
My blessings are all around.
Love and comfort which I do not deserve,
Are beside me to be found.

With joy and pain, I face each night
Both of which I perceive.
Tomorrow comes as the dawn breaks light.
And pride in the quest I've achieved.

L.M Haddow

The Storm

The storm around us gathers.
Times of anguish and of strain.
Where believing is a hardship.
Dreaming causes pain.

Roads are filled with fog.
The gloom and sombre night.
The battle that's within us.
To dance within the light.

Clouds gather full of rain drops.
And thunder invades the sky.
Our days are heavy with longing.
Tears within our sigh.

No matter where we turn.
The trek is whole with sorrow.
And we search for that horizon.
To take us to tomorrow.

And the enemy amongst us.
From our own regret it does derive.
We allow it to take over.
And within it, do survive.

We shield the world from moments.
That we cannot share with them.
We pretend the darkness is freeing.
And guard it, like a gem.

It's hard to impart the sadness.
That we walk with through-out life.
Words don't do it justice.
Nor show the hurt and strife.

But we are all around you.
We stand near you today.
It's only that our shadows.
Are hidden, far away.

We smile through that storm.
That rages deep below
And keep our sorrow hidden.
Our heartache, and our woe.

L.M Haddow

<u>Strength</u>

Sometimes in life things can be tough
And our own inner strength just isn't enough
So, God in his Wisdom gave to us all
Family and Friends to help ease any fall

And with those people are hands to hold
Worries to share and burdens to off load
For in these people who are always around
The strength we all lack is there to be found

So, I send this to you, so you will know
That no matter the journey you are never alone
And when that mountain seems too high to climb
In your loved ones a hand and prayer you will find.

L.M Haddow

<u>Enough is enough</u>

Okay so the pain is a ten,
And today I just can't stand up.
But yesterday was the same as this.
So surely enough is enough.

The toilet and shower are mountains to climb.
And I dress with the speed of a snail.
Surely, I've served my sentence in life,
And it's time I succeed and not fail.

I am tired of being so slow when I move.
Or needing such aid when I sit.
I don't mean to sound like pain in the ass,
But I've had it up to here, with this shit!

So, when is the dawn coming for me?
Must I wait for another whole year?
Because the pain is taking my sparkle away,
And to forget who I am is my fear.

Bring me my rainbow or that star from the North.
And stop with the messing around.
I learnt to be grateful for all that I have,
The blessings in me have been found.

L.M Haddow

<u>Who I am?</u>

My health it does not define me.
It is not my everything.
And though it is a hardship.
It's not the song I sing.

People may see me altered.
With such pain in my eyes.
But trust me I'm still here.
Standing in your sighs.

So, when you stop to talk
And wonder what to say.
Please remember our conversation
On another day.

When I was not ill or fragile.
When you laughed with me right there.
Please try hard to talk.
About something other than care.

I know you are good hearted.
And want to wish me fine.
But I want to discuss the gossip.
And laugh with eyes that shine.

My humour is still with me.
My talent is still too.
There's so much more about me.
That I want to say to you.

I live with doctor appointments.
I know you want to know.
But after the first questions,
Let our chatter grow.

I am more than just my health.
Because let me tell you now.
My ability is stronger.
Than my disability would allow.

L.M Haddow

Standing on a Cliff Edge

I am standing on a cliff edge.
The fall I see beyond.
I wonder if I jump.
The pain will all be gone.

I am walking through a forest.
With a rope tied round my waist.
I cannot run or leave it.
I am bounded to this place.

I am drowning in the darkness.
My thoughts are my own foes.
I am left with only sorrow.
Trouble, doubt and woe.

My hands no longer keep me.
Safe from my own fear.
No longer can they comfort.
Nor wipe my falling tear.

My memory it is fading.
My sparkle long since lost.
The words that are within me.
Are taken with a cost.

The steps I take now closer.
To the edge on which I stand
The wonder of the freedom.
When I quietly land.

And yet I know within me.
That backwards I must walk.
To find a different pathway.
To find a different rock.

Untie the rope around me.
Let the pain explode.
Believe my heart is stronger.
To find a braver road.

L.M Haddow

Always believe in your Fairy tale.

For the Children

Monsters

Is there a monster under my bed?
I climb the stairs with pending dread.
Will he pop out and give a roar?
I peek my head around the door.

Is there a monster in my room?
That only appears in the gloom?
Will I sleep right through the night?
Or will I wake with a sudden fright?

Is there a monster big and strong?
Waiting for me all day long?
To come out when the sun goes down,
With an angry, scary, horrible frown?

Is there a monster? I must find out.
I must be left with no doubt.
Is there a monster waiting for me?
I am sure there really cannot be.

If there's a monster – its' time to know.
And I will tell him – "off you go".
I will be brave and have a peek,
No matter that my knees feel weak.

There is no monster under my bed.
I had a look and he must have fled.
He saw me coming big and tough,
And off he went in a huff.

Now the monster is truly gone,
I say to myself with a yawn.
So, into my bed I happily get,
Monster free no need to fret.

L.M Haddow

In the night

On the hall clock midnight does chime,
Down from the bed silently they climb.
With a whirl of sparkles and magic jive,
The toys of the house have come alive.

Softly stirring they stretch and yawn.
Slowly to life they are mystically drawn.
Through a power that is hard to construe,
Gathered together form a wondrous crew.

Old Teddy Bear, scruffy from loving.
From nightly kisses and constant hugging.
Kindly smile and a twinkle in his eye.
He awakes with a funny roar like sigh.

Sweet Dolly dimple with golden locks,
Blue patched pinafore and pure white socks.
She rubs her eyes to bring her round.
And smiles at her friends without a sound.

The doll house in the corner of the room.
Has come to light amidst the gloom.
Inside each wooden sweet wee doll,
Looks out the windows and waves to all.

The racing cars, red, green and black.
Start their engines on their ambitious track.
With a wave of the flag off they fly,
Whizzing and zooming quickly by.

The red coated soldiers start to talk,
And out springs good old jack in the box.
The action figures stand bold and strong,
Ready for fun the whole night long.

From the colourful large toy box,
Out comes bunny and Fredrick Fox.
Molly Mouse and Mickey as well.
And Henry tortoise with his shell.

As when the clock strikes on the twelve,
They can awake and be themselves.
To dance and sing, laugh and play,
Until the moment of break of day.

And slowly as the dawn shows light
So, ends the magic bewitching night.
The toys asleep they all do fall
Each teddy, race car and dancing doll.

L.M Haddow

Best Friends

Perhaps you may think I'm bad.
But my Sister drives me mad.
She never lets me in her room.
And always makes me grump and fume.

She never lets me play her games.
Often, she even calls me names.
She never lets me near her toys.
And always says I'm making noise.

My Sister and I can often fight.
Mostly because she knows I'm right!
She never ever does give in.
Or simply ever let me win.

My Sister says I am a pain.
And always says I am to blame.
She and I will never agree.
I wish she would just let me be.

But to us, Mum once advised.
One day we would be so surprised.
And, she said, that we would see.
Without each other we could not be.

We'll love each other from our heart.
Always together, even when apart.
On each other we will depend.
On our Sister – our best friend.

And how, I ask, does Mum know this?
That we will grow and have such bliss?
What makes her sure with no doubt?
That it will truly all work out?

And Mum she smiles and says to me.
How she knows what will be.
"Though we argued and had a rant,
My Best Friend is now your Aunt".

L.M Haddow

Spots

I was a lovely child.
My Mother used to say.
Sweet and kind and loving.
Adorable in my play.

Then one day it happened.
I am not still sure what.
But I woke up in the morning.
And discovered my first spot.

My head it rages often.
My mood will bring you down.
I can't be bothered with you.
My smile is now a frown.

I hate my whole daft wardrobe.
I have nothing that I like.
I lost my love for dollies.
Or skateboard and my bike.

I have no clue what's unfolding.
Yesterday seemed so clear.
Today I find me fussy.
With no joy or cheer.

So, I must find out the answer.
On why my life has changed.
Why the way I'm feeling.
Makes me feel deranged?

My Mother she informs me.
With kindness she does allow.
"My Darling little monster,
A teenager you are now"!

L.M Haddow

Old red Sledge

Two little girls up the hill they go.
Leaving footprints in the snow.
Crisp and fresh, clear and bright.
A landscape covered in pure white.

Little girls - one blonde, one dark.
Climbing in the silent park.
No-one's around they're all alone.
Even the birds south have flown.

Up they climb higher still.
Despite the cold winters chill.
On they march – the scale is high.
Reaching almost to the sky.

And they haul behind their backs.
An old red sledge leaving tracks.
Not one sound does it make.
Covered in soft snow flakes.

The little girls their task is great.
To soar so high, their legs they ache.
But on they go, with silent brawn.
To the top they are firmly drawn.

As they arrive it's high for sure.
The ground below so obscure.
Distant views - so far beyond.
Of Fields and trees and the pond.

And at the top they get prepared.
Neither one is slightly scared.
Balanced surely on the edge.
Their place their dear red old sledge.

In they climb cuddled so close.
The cold air now biting their nose.
Get ready set - off they fly.
And the world starts zooming by.

A rush of air - so icy cold.
Both are so very bold.
Faster, faster they do descend.
Without a clue where they'll end.

Laughter rings from their throats.
Across the snow they quickly float.
With the shouts of screams of cheer.
They twist and pull, trying to steer.

And at last the end they reach.
With a sudden, fun filled screech.
upside down both they land.
And help each other up to stand.

What a journey of pure delight.
From such a steep and scary height.
It was a joy and such fun.
But now the entertainments done.

But not for long they both comply.
And off they set with a sigh.
Up the Hill they start again.
Two wee girls, two best friends.

L.M Haddow

Fairy Dreams

In the Sky the stars shine bright.
Twinkle Twinkle with magical light.
Boys and Girls are all tucked up in bed.
Warm and cosy, sweet dreams in their head.

And in the Forest the Bunnies sleep sound.
Foxes and Badgers in dens in the ground.
No Creatures are stirring – not even the deer
All are asleep – or so it would appear….

For deep in the Forest – far from view.
Are Balloons and cake and Music too.
Tonight, is the night of the Fairy Ball
And everyone is welcome – one and all.

Wings that Sparkle - Colours bright.
It is indeed a wondrous sight.
Softly floating through the trees.
As gentle as a summers breeze.

Dandelion Sweets and Pumpkin Pop.
A Pixie band that totally Rocks.
Tiny laughter and party games.
Magical Candles with dancing flames.

And on a thrown made of sparkles and Pearls
Is the Fairy Queen with golden curls.
Kind and good with a watchful eye.
She watches her fairies flying by

Now how to get to the Fairy Fun.
It is a secret – here's how it's done.
You must be good, climb into bed.
And on your pillow, rest your head.

Say your Prayers and kiss Goodnight.
Only then you'll see the Fairies Lights
In your dreams – where wishes come true.
You'll fly to the party – they are waiting for you

L.M Haddow

Land Ahoy!!

"I will be the Captain" – Andy said.
With Eye patch and hat on his head.
I'll be in charge on that you can bank.
And if anyone argues you'll walk the plank.

On my mighty ship you'll be my crew.
And we will sail the seven seas so blue.
We will see so many far away islands.
Seek such treasures, with lots of diamonds.

Steady as she goes - watch those sails.
Swimming besides us, dolphins and whales.
Swab the decks and the guns to man.
I will show you how my ship is ran.

In my hand is my amazing sword.
Now do as I say, or you'll be overboard.
Across the ocean we shall explore.
And may even fight in a mighty war.

Yo-ho-ho and a bottle of rum.
I will show you all how it's done.
Aboard my vessel – land ahoy.
The rowing boats – now deploy.

Out on the sea the waves are strong.
But my crew keep rowing on.
To the beach – do you wonder?
What treasures we now will plunder?

Almost there – keep on my crew.
Amazing adventures are waiting for you.
Such wonders I promise - you all will see.
Oh, we have to stop Mum says it's time for tea.

Okay my gang we will proceed.
Once we have had a mighty feed.
As all strong pirates need to rest.
So, they can be at their best.

Now lunch is over, what a feast.
Now onwards men towards the East.
The adventure has only just begun.
Being a Pirate is such fun.

L.M Haddow

Messy David

"Now little David that room is a mess!
I am not best pleased – can you guess?"
His Mummy said with an awful moan
"Clothes and toys in a heap just thrown"

"Little David - I ask you why
Can't you just put things by?
Once you are finished with your toy
Why are you such a messy boy?"

"On the floor the jigsaw puzzles.
All the pieces in such muddles.
The drawing pencils from the other day.
Why haven't you just put them away?"

"And My David who I love no doubt,
There is something else I must point out.
That bugs belong in the garden free
Not in a jar beside your TV"

"But more of a concern than all the Jumble,
Is the worry that you could take a tumble.
Just getting from the door to the bed.
I must say this is something I dread"

"So, my Darling – my precious son.
Don't feel I wish to spoil your fun.
But something really must improve.
And all this mess must be removed"

L.M Haddow

My Oak tree

In our Garden stands an old Oak tree.
I'm pretty sure it's there just for me.
Although the birds tend to rest.
In its branches, in their nest.

And yes, the squirrels one also finds.
Have the same turn of mind.
That the tree is their own home.
No matter where they tend to roam.

But you see - I have to say.
To me it seems a different way.
That even though I let them share.
That old tree's mine, for me it's there.

Its branches are so thick and strong.
It's never tired all day long.
Even when I climb and swing.
It stands so strong through everything.

And here's the thing about my tree.
It becomes whatever I wish it to be.
A rocket ship that goes to the stars.
Speeding past Pluto and past Mars.

I can be on a large pirate's ship.
Or in a lion's den with my whip.
Go anywhere, go so far.
Driving in a racing car.

It is my land of make believe.
There's nothing that it cannot be.
And yes, my tree is always there.
In rain, or when the weather's fair.

And so, I say to my wooden friend.
Whose branches hold and never bend.
Thank you for those special days.
Which on you I happily played.

L.M Haddow

School days

"Well wee girls how was your day?"
They heard their Mummy softly say.
After school had come to a close.
Looking at their wrinkled clothes.

Messy hair and dirty scuffed shoes.
"Oh goodness what happened to you?
This morning, when you were last seen,
You were oh so fresh and oh so clean".

"But I admit" Mummy said with a sigh.
With a smile and a twinkling eye
"It looks as though now your day is done,
You had loads of giggles and lots of fun".

"But please little girls do try your best,
To remember how you should be dressed.
And try to stay a bit more neat.
From your heads to your sweet wee feet"

"I know that school is a busy place,
With games to play and friends to chase.
But if you could just take a break.
From trying to make Mums head ache".

"Because now I know my night ahead,
While you two monsters are warm in bed.
My job will be with such woe,
Clothes to wash and buttons to sow"

"But my Darlings I must confess,
That I was the same at making a mess.
And Grannie also often said.
You naughty girl – now off to bed".

"So, I will smile and let it go.
But this I must let you know.
That tomorrow is a brand-new day.
Oh yes and Grannie is coming to stay!"

L.M Haddow

Training wheels

Here I sit on my bike.
With no training wheels in sight.
Today's the day - this I know.
I really hope Dad doesn't let go.

Slowly the peddles start to turn.
Hang on a second – this may be fun.
No wait, am scared - what if I fall?
Or ride straight into the garden wall?

Dad says take a moment and be brave.
He'll be there If I need to be saved.
There is nothing to fear – it will be fine.
Just start off slow and take my time.

Okay let's go – and off I start.
With such a thumping in my heart.
Every turn I feel really unsteady.
I simply know I'm so not ready.

But after just seconds go passed.
Suddenly - I am flying fast.
Still with caution, but not as fearful.
And yes, I say - almost cheerful.

Hurray for me – I've passed the test.
I took a chance and tried my best.
So now I can ride my lovely bike.
With no training wheels in sight!

L.M Haddow

<u>Over the Rainbow</u>

There is a place, in stories old.
That's full of joy and glittering gold.
It's in your dreams, far away.
Over the Rainbow, some do say.

It's where all dreams do come true.
It's full of grace and beauty too.
Where fairies live and Unicorns thrive.
Where Fairy-tales come alive.

And if you believe in what may be.
Then this world of magic, you will see.
It's not a journey, not too far.
Just look above and find your star.

Cause inside of you is a gift.
For some today is adrift.
But if you look deep inside.
Your imagination cannot be denied.

With it you are free to fly.
Amongst the cloud's way up high.
Be whatever you dream to be.
Without your phone or your TV.

Let your imagination loose.
And all that it may induce.
Always let your dreams take flight.
And find that land with Fairy light.

L.M Haddow

With Every new adventure, brings colours to your dreams.

Holidays &
Celebrations
& New Journeys

<u>*Your new home*</u>

May your new Home bring you a future of charm.
May it shelter you both from darkness and harm.
This place where your kin all now abide.
May it be full of love, happiness and pride.

But hold your memories safe in your heart.
Keeping us close - even when we're apart.
And this place you now leave - may you ever know,
Will always be part of you wherever you go.

So, we send you away with all our affection.
And thank you for the never-ending connection.
And are grateful that we are so lucky to say.
Our lives have been blessed by knowing you today.

So, a grace we offer on your new dwelling.
May life's new adventure now be excelling.
And the hope that we send offer good substance.
For a life full of peace, joy and abundance.

May your new home offer calming peace.
And may all your stresses now please cease.
May it bring you at times much needed rest.
And may you and your clan always be blessed.

L.M Haddow

Twas a Scottish night before Christmas

"Emma and Abby now it's time for bed".
With a twinkle in her eye, their Mummy said.
"No messing about, no time for delay.
Cause you know tomorrow is Christmas day".

"Some biscuits and a dram are all laid out.
For Santa to find and sooth any drought.
A carrot for Rudolph to keep him right.
For his long and wondrous, magical flight".

"The stockings are hung for Santa to find.
To fill with presents – he's ever so kind
To my Lassies with dreams in their heads.
Now come on Wee Lambs – off to bed".

"Emma and Abby, close your eyes.
When you awake a wondrous surprise.
For tomorrow's a day of magic delight.
Now off to sleep. I love you night night".

Both little girls now tucked up in bed.
With dreams of Santa in their wee heads.
When awake they both jump with a sudden fright.
And peer out the door into the night.

A noise from downstairs – what they don't know.
Perhaps back to bed they simply should go.
But little girls one often does find.
Mischievous thoughts go through their wee minds.

To the top of the stairs silently they creep.
Just a quick look – just a wee peek.
Not that they want to spoil the surprise.
But jings help ma boab they can't believe their eyes.

For whom do you think they find standing there?
Right by the tree laying presents with care.
Good old Saint Nick, but jings what a sight.
A red kilt he is wearing – what a braw delight.

With rosy cheeks and a big tartan sack.
A silver buckle and a floppy red hat.
A sporran underneath that shines with gold.
A right Scottish Santa if the truth be told.

He turns with a smile and spies the wee tots.
Often for Santa this happens a lot.
Wee lads or wee lassies pop doon to see.
Old Santa laying presents under the tree.

And he gives them a wink and ever so fast.
He drains the dram and puts down the glass.
With a click of his fingers he's suddenly gone.
To the next house, he must, quickly move on.

Both Emma and Abby giggle with glee.
How can they explain what they did see?
That Santa's a Scot and a bonnie one at that.
And frankly they didn't find him all that fat.

Back up to bed quickly they run.
And whisper to each other about the fun.
A secret we'll keep – no-one we'll tell.
And off to sleep the Bairns they fell.

And high up above on the Pollok clan roof.
Came the sounds of bells and reindeer hooves.
Up and away to the next house he flew.
Wishing all a braw Christmas and a lucky one too.

L.M Haddow

High School

Moments have gone by.
And the years have flown.
It amazes me,
How much you've grown.

And now the time has come.
The day to embark.
On a brand-new beginning.
A brand-new start.

And I know how it feels.
To start somewhere new.
Nerves and excitement.
And some fears too.

But always remember
In the girl that you are.
Beautiful and strong.
A bright shining star.

And also remember,
How much you are loved.
That your family is here.
In times good and tough.

And on this first step
In a new grown up sphere.
May your journey be with love.
And always with good cheer.

My perfect Darling daughter.
So sweet and so lovely.
Always so kind.
So caring and bubbly.

May god bless your days.
Tomorrow and forever
And may the beauty in your heart.
Leave you never.

L.M Haddow

Weird street

Tonight, our street looks strangely weird.
Ghost, goblins and things to be feared.
Walking about – all calm and bold,
It's very odd if truth be told.

I saw a Witch and a monster too.
Even a lion from the zoo.
A pussy cat with a long black tail,
And yes, there goes a giant snail.

There is a vampire, looks so real.
And a spider that makes me squeal.
There's a knight with sword and shield.
And a Scarecrow who is from a field.

I see a zombie that moans and groans.
And a skeleton with old white bones.
There goes a princess in her gown.
And a funny, scary looking clown.

Now I can't be sure, but it seems to me,
That something bizarre appears to be.
Going on outside on this cold dark night.
All of this does not seem quite right.

So, I ask My Mum – what's proceeding?
Cause this outlook is quite misleading.
She smiles at me and explains the scene,
"Tonight, My Dear is Halloween"

L.M Haddow

Father's Day for Father in Law

I came into your family.
By the bonds of wedding vows.
You welcomed me with open arms.
With all that love allows.

And as a Daughter of your clan.
On this Father's Day.
I wish you to know my gratitude.
In my own particular way.

I married your eldest boy.
To walk with him through life.
You embraced me with joy and love
As his brand-new wife.

I know my blessings is thanks to you.
And the superb job you have done.
By raising my amazing husband
The man that is your son.

And today my Dear Father in law.
I promise this to you.
I will always be by his side.
My love for him is true.

And to your Darling Family.
Of which I am proud to belong.
I will always be loyal and fair.
Trustworthy and strong.

So, thank you for all you are.
And all I know you do.
For every smile and every hug.
Simply for being you.

L.M Haddow

Holiday recipe

The recipe for Christmas.
The way to get it right.
Take a house build for four,
And fill it for the night.

Take one moody teenager.
And children full of sweets.
Mix it in with tiredness,
And bring it slow to heat.

Sprinkle in resentment,
An argument from long ago.
Add a mix of alcohol.
And watch the pressure grow.

Add in laughter and some tears.
And a ton of Christmas food.
Bake at high till overdone.
Until well and truly stewed.

Cool it down, with a pinch of wine.
Stir in Christmas cheer.
Dust a dash of amnesia.
And repeat it all next year.

L.M Haddow

Happy Birthday

A Birthday is a day.
That a blessing is sent to you.
To bring you joy and laughter.
Today and all year through.

A Birthday is a moment.
That love ones take the time.
To say their warmest thank you.
For being our friend so fine.

So today is your day.
And with us you celebrate.
A reminder that this year.
Is the year to do, not to wait.

Cherish everyday
With the joy you feel right now.
Find that star to wish upon.
And all your dreams allow.

L.M Haddow

Leaving home

When I was little.
My Grannie used to say.
One day when –
One special day.

I would find my path,
And start my quest.
To a life that would take me.
To another nest.

She talked of teachings,
That I would grasp.
And dreams and stars.
That I would clasp.

She said that life,
Offers crusades.
That brings adventure.
Joy and parades.

And she said I must,
Cherish her lesson.
And know that family,
Is always a blessing.

Cause we are together.
Even when we're apart.
We carry each other.
In our heart.

So, I tell you this message.
My Grannie relayed.
In the hope that it brings you,
Some comforting aid.

When they look at the stars,
When they are far away.
Remember we look,
Upon the same stars today.

And the bonds of family,
No distance can divide.
Not when there's love,
Devotion and pride.

And the wonder of family,
What is remarkably true.
They always know,
Home is with you.

L.M Haddow

Every Butterfly is a creation of Love

Religious & spiritual

Lift up your eyes

"Lift up your eyes
And look on the fields"
Smell the fragrance that,
The wild flower yields.

For all the bounty.
And food there grows.
The beauty and wonder,
Of the precious rose.

May our thanks be given,
With a moment of thought.
For those whose lives,
Have struggle and fraught.

So, let us be thankful,
What the Lord has provided.
Praise be his wonder.
And his love undivided.

L.M Haddow

The soul of the Church

The mist that lingers,
On a Sunday Morn.
Around the resting place,
Of Generations gone.

The bells are ringing.
No time to delay.
The service is starting,
On God's Holy day.

Hymns we will start,
Joyous voices raise.
The Church is awake,
To sing God's praise.

The whisper of Prayers,
From young and from old.
The pulpit high standing,
God's message is told.

This building is more,
Than bricks and wood.
It's a temple of safety,
Of blessings and good.

Elders of past,
And children of today.
Same message is heard,
And treasured the same way.

The Church is formed,
On connection's so true.
The loved ones that gather,
God's love shines through.

Praise be to God
For building this place.
And for bringing us here
To share in his grace.

L.M Haddow

Children of the Church

We are the children of the fold.
We are the future for all to behold.
We stand here today in our holy place.
Saying words of peace and of grace.

We are the voice that tomorrow will know.
Spreading Gods word so his herd may grow.
We are the lambs that will thrive into sheep.
To carry on the Church and traditions we'll keep.

For what you have brought the Youth of this Kirk.
We thank you for all your pure hard work.
You have given to us the tools to embrace.
The world outside with strength and grace.

And we are proud to say that thanks to you.
The lessons we'll carry our whole life through.
For taking the time and knowing that we.
Are as important as important truly can be.

For saying to the world – these are the ones.
They are tomorrow's daughters and sons.
It is they that will carry on our family's soul.
So, we must teach them all that we know.

And we know at times we make some clatter.
And for some that really does so matter.
And sitting still isn't always our strength.
For all the church full sermons length.

But do not doubt our love for our Mission.
We promise to cherish all future additions.
And continue your work after you're gone.
And ensure that your legacy lives on.

So, in our hands you can leave with peace.
Knowing for sure we will never cease.
To honour your work and continue it on.
Into the futures brand new dawn.

L.M Haddow

My Faith

Where is your church?
That you sing praise?
Is it within four walls,
On a holy day?

Is in by the Sea,
On a cliff top far?
Is in the night?
Gazing on a star?

What is your faith?
That others judge?
Does it have to be?
"God is Love"

Is it to you perhaps,
A different route?
That doesn't look,
To the holy book?

Is it in the love?
Of those close by?
Is it in your lovers?
Passionate sigh?

Does it stand against?
The test of time?
Does it keep you safe?
On that mountain you climb?

For me my Faith,
Is a private grace.
It gives me peace.
Joy and brace.

It does not cover.
A religious sect.
Nor has strict rules,
That must be met.

It is within me.
It's my love and hope.
That tomorrow comes,
And I will cope.

Do not judge,
Some others truth.
Live your life,
As you know you should.

Never wonder,
Where do, they pray?
Let them find
Their own sacred way.

L.M Haddow

Our Minister, Our Friend

The Path our life takes us –
is always by Gods hand.
The route he draws to follow,
is a clear and careful plan.

And often in our lives
we meet people on the way.
That he has sent to guide us
and help us through each day.

And the Lord he knew our Parish,
a Teacher we did pursue.
To bring to us his Holy word
and worship with us too.

To us he sent a Preacher,
for times of joy and times of pain.
To guide us in our questions
and lessen moments of strain.

Now Gods Plan is changing –
and your paths a different way.
Before you go and leave us,
there's something we must say.

In you we got a teacher
that performed his duties grand.
But we also found a valued friend,
a kind and loving man.

So, as you now depart
and begin a new planned quest
Know that because of you -
our lives are truly blessed.

Our love - please take with you,
and though we are apart.
The lessons that you taught us –
we carry in our heart.

L.M Haddow

Adam and Eve

God, he said to Adam…
"Now listen here my Son"
I have some rules to tell you.
But here's the crucial one".

"See that tree there yonder?
The one with all the fruit.
If you're feeling peckish,
Plan another route".

"You can eat from any other,
Take and have your fill.
But that one trees a no go.
Be done and that's my will".

"Okay" said Adam calmly.
"For me I'll stay away.
From the tree you mentioned.
I will honour what you say".

Now here is where our story,
Gets a tad confused.
We are told that lovely Eve,
Was the one who was accused

Of tempting our dear Adam,
With the apple red and hot.
Of taking a bite right out the side,
When God has told them not

But as a Woman I must admit.
That men they can tell tales.
And let's be clear we weren't there,
To check the full details.

My theory goes, my own idea.
That Adam was the one,
That took the bite and turn to Eve
And said, "oh boy yum yum"

When God he checked and saw the deed.
He was so vexed and grieved.
And Adam answered as all men do.
It wasn't me, it was our Eve!

And thus began that manly trait,
The fibs they all do tell.
And yet they wonder often why,
Women tend to yell.

So, here's the lesson, from me to you.
And please have no doubt.
That men can have a bit of bother,
Getting the truth right out.

But one point for the men out there.
All grateful you shouid be.
When God he said get out my house,
With Adam, Eve did flee.

So always be kind to her.
Who often does comply.
And remember boys she always knows,
Each time you tell a lie!

L.M Haddow

Tenderly tight

The Lord he gave me sense.
For me to choose my way.
Yet his loving hand still guides me
Every single day.

The Lord he gave me joy,
With Family and with friends.
Yet his presence is the greatest,
His loyalty never bends.

The Lord he lets me ask,
All questions on my mind.
And brings to me the answers,
To leave all doubt behind.

The Lord he never leaves me,
In both day or night.
His loving arms around me,
Firm and tenderly tight.

And though this world leaves me,
With burdens I must bear.
The Lord his love surrounds me,
His gentle loving care.

L.M Haddow

<u>Hold your dreams</u>

Take the spirit that's within you.
Dance within its light.
Hold your dreams forever.
Let your heart take flight.

Always be stronger.
Than the world may let you be.
Never doubt your passion.
Or the truth that sets you free.

Who you are is amazing.
Though the world may not agree.
But always stand for the truth inside.
And never hide nor flee.

If they doubt or mock you.
Or question who you are.
Remember you're what God made you.
Unique, like every star.

Let it be their problem.
If they live a different way.
Always tell them proudly.
You are here and here to stay.

L.M Haddow

Let your dreams take flight.

Other Moments

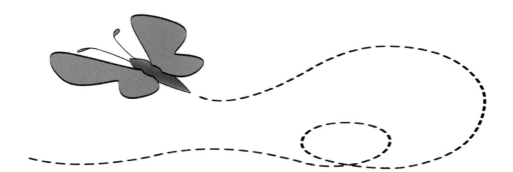

Decades of colour

The painting of life through dreams and each star.
Flowing with colours – makes us who we are.
The tapestry of living and the touch of another,
Be it lover or friend, Father or Mother.

Dreams of tomorrow with memories of the past.
Designing and painting – the colours to last.
Moulding and forming a part of one's soul.
Leaving the world, a little more whole.

Every decade that pass, the colours they change,
Some can be wondrous, some dark with much pain.
But every moment that the colours are painted there,
Brings a new memory of life and love to share

Each year the colours flow - offers new age,
And the scenery changes on life's keen stage.
The colours may be softer and slightly lined,
But for sure they are far wiser inclined.

And the story the painting it tells the sphere,
Is one of journeys, with love and good cheer.
The colours embrace each dream and each chase.
Every moment it cherishes, with joy and true grace.

May your painting continue to be a joyous work of art.
May your memories continue to be held in your heart.
And May God bless your colours and all that you are,
Every shade, every dream, every moment, every star.

L.M Haddow

Clouds

The darkness in the clouds.
Gather in our heart.
The fear that in tomorrow.
Pain or worry starts.

The journey on the highway.
Though the storm does strong blow.
Is the path that life can take us.
And the walk is hard and slow.

The sunshine is within us.
The love we hold so dear.
The way forward is the only.
Route to end the fear.

Take the clouds that surround you.
And blow them all away.
Know that strength is your saviour
No matter come what may.

And when the clouds are drowning.
Our will to carry through.
Know the force to carry onwards.
Lies only within you.

Believe in the sunshine.
Fight through the storm with grace.
Take your heart and walk with vigour.
To that sun kissed place.

L.M Haddow

This dear auld House

This house stands often empty and alone.
With only memories of days now gone.
Whispers in the untouched space.
Spirits giving love, peace and grace.

In this house so much laughter rang.
Tears were cried and songs were sang.
Grief was felt and fights were started.
Love was made and souls were parted.

And as for me - my memories here.
Are still so bonnie, strong and clear.
With warm Peat fires and water fights.
Lively breakfasts and peaceful nights.

Pictures painted and ringing school bells.
Crossword puzzles and Thurso sea shells.
Braw tattie soup, and the many cats.
Having a bevvy - a laugh and a chat.

This house gave at times much needed rest.
And parties that were simply the best.
This house offered often calming peace.
And here my strivings always ceased.

And those who visit fae outside our clan.
New memories for you have now began.
Although don't be feart - but listen true.
Cause our voices can be still heard through.

And even though we are not always here.
And new generations now come each year.
I know that even when we are far away.
The Pollok souls are now here tae stay.

L.M Haddow

The light within us

There are moments in our life.
That take us to the wall.
Stages that define us.
And lessons when we fall.

We stand within our energy.
Be it strong or hard to clasp.
We take each step onwards.
And hold within our grasp.

And when the journey is lonely.
The road never seems to bend.
We must carry forward.
Until the awaking ends.

So, hold the will to march.
And take each step with pride.
Cause in those darken moments,
Is light to be our guide.

L.M Haddow

<u>My Homeland</u>

The heather on the moors.
The never-ending land.
Moments I have lived here.
Amongst my Gaelic Clan.

The loch that shines like sunshine.
The air that holds the sea.
My memories they are held here.
Souring, wild and free.

The distant voices calling.
Across the barren scope.
Full of mystic wonder.
Of passion and of hope.

My heart is in the Highlands.
This land of stark outlook.
Its beauty is within me.
My soul, it long since took.

Stay True my peaceful homeland.
I will always hold you fond.
And shelter there forever.
My Highland, loyal bond.

L.M Haddow

Summer

Smell the air of a summer wind.
Float amongst the splendour.
Hold a cloud in your grasp.
Let your mind surrender.

Walk the river bank with ease.
Live amongst its heartbeat.
Feel the warmth of the sun.
Gentle, rays so sweet.

Touch the grass in the field.
And dance amidst the flowers.
Hold your face to the sky.
And feel the summer showers.

Breathe in the life all around.
Let your senses fly.
Be a part of the world.
As Summer days go by

L.M Haddow

The Butterfly

The butterfly is born.
From a hard and lonely shell.
Awakes her lovely wings.
And adorns us with her spell.

Her colours are unique.
Her wings express her soul.
Her journey from the battle.
Brings beauty from her flow.

She sees the world as freedom.
Her life has now begun.
To fly amongst the daylight.
To bathe within the sun.

The Butterfly's a jewel.
That lives amongst us haste
Leaving with her moments.
That bring us peace and grace.

L.M Haddow

Gentle Purr

People don't understand,
Why I love you so.
To them you are just a pet.
Though cute they all do know.

Folks they think I am mad.
That my Children you are mine.
That I cherish you, as all Mums do.
With all my heart and time.

To me you are my babies.
You need love and comfort right.
Cuddles and affection.
Tucked in and kissed goodnight.

People just don't grasp,
The void that I once knew.
Before my babies came to me.
Before I fell for you.

And you have given me such love.
Filled that void within my heart
You look to me as your Mum.
Never shall we part.

Always my little souls.
My children with soft fur.
My heart it sours to feel you near.
To hear your gentle purr.

So, let them laugh and mock at me.
At what I say and do.
They'd give the world, I know for sure.
To be allowed to cuddle you.

L.M Haddow

The lass

Och lassie that stands in the' glen,
Wi' locks the' colour o' gold.
Yer fightin' spirit in yer een.
Yer hert true 'n' bold.

Ye haud the' bairn tae yer breast,
and keep the' dwelling clean.
Ye tak' the' pain that life kin serve,
And face it strong and keen.

The' hert o' a lass runs sae deep.
Her secrets hid fae sicht.
She is the' braun of' the' clan,
It's love that keeps her richt.

Sae kneel afore the' lass o' yers,
Be it daughter, mither or wife.
She is the' light of the' world,
Thro' sorrow, joy 'n' strife.

L.M Haddow

These Women

These women in my life.
The ones from which I've grown.
Shaped me and encourage.
All my life I've known.

My Grandmothers both true.
In their different ways.
My Mother and my Sister.
With me all my days.

My Best Friend, my heart.
Her love it knows no scope.
With me in good moments.
In sadness, my life rope.

My Aunt who was my person.
On whom I could depend.
Was more than just an Auntie.
Was a true, real Friend.

These women in my life.
Their knowledge and their strength.
Made me who I am today.
For all my Journeys length.

L.M Haddow

Memories

Memories I have gathered,
Though always held sincere
Colours of our yesterday –
Cherished and so dear.

Moments of our days –
Together and apart
Given here in this book,
Always in my heart.

Souls that have now parted
And stages now in the past
But here is captured forever more,
Images to last.

Stories of the journeys,
Travelled through-out time
All the hearts I have known,
Forever will be mine.

Stars not always followed,
Though still wished upon
Fairy tales of our life,
Seasons past and gone.

Each page is filled with love and peace,
Blessings for always
For memories that are still to come.
For all our cherished days.

L.M Haddow

I hope you liked my book,
And it touched you in the heart.
I hope you found it moving,
And loving from the start.

And I hope that even just,
One verse it made you smile.
My efforts in sharing this,
Have been so worthwhile.

Till next time

Louise x

Bonnie & Clyde Creations

21884916R00061

Printed in Great Britain
by Amazon